Christmas Customs

Written by DENNIS MILLER
Illustrated by HELEN DRABBLE

Ladybird Books

Christmas

What does it mean to you? Cards and presents, good things to eat, trimmings and decorations, carols and nativity plays, crackers and pantomimes?

The word Christmas means *Christ's Mass*. The Mass is an ancient Christian church service at which people give praise and glory to God. Christians believe that Jesus Christ was born in a stable in Bethlehem about two thousand years ago and was the Son of God.

Religious customs

The story of Jesus' birth explains many of the things we see and do at Christmas time. It explains why we sing carols about Jesus, and why we sometimes put a star on top of the Christmas tree, like the star the three Wise Men followed. It explains why we put on nativity plays, why we make Christmas cribs and why we give presents, just as the Wise Men gave gifts to Jesus.

Carols

Carol, which comes from the same Greek word as *chorus*, used to mean a round song or dance, or chorus of joy. There are Midsummer carols, Easter carols, May carols – even November carols – as well as Christmas carols, which are songs about the birth of Jesus.

St Francis's Christmas crib

When St Francis of Assisi made the first Christmas crib, hundreds of years ago in Italy, crowds of people came to see it. He tethered an ox and an ass by a rocky cave in the woods and real people acted the parts of Mary and Joseph. St Francis put a wax doll in the manger to represent Jesus. Christmas cribs have been popular ever since.

The winter festivals

Many of our Christmas customs began long before Jesus was born. In ancient times the sun was sometimes worshipped as a god. Christmas Day falls in the middle of winter when there is little sun and the days are short. Pagans lit sacred fires and held ceremonies at this time of year, hoping to give the sun back its strength.

The Saturnalia

The people of ancient Rome worshipped the sun, and they honoured *Saturn* as the god of all growing things. His special festival was held in mid winter, when the Romans decorated their homes with *evergreen* branches to remind Saturn to send crops and plants for food the following spring.

The days of this festival were called the Saturnalia, and it was the custom to give evergreen branches as presents. Little clay dolls were also specially made and sold for people to give to one another.

For most people, the Saturnalia was a time of fun and joy. But many people found it an unhappy occasion. Often, there were animal sacrifices. As time went by, more and more people became Christians and stopped worshipping Saturn and the sun. In winter they began instead to remember the birth of Jesus, the Son of their God.

St Lucy's day in Sweden

In the fourth century St Lucy was killed for her faith in Jesus. Legend says that after her death she became a bright star in the sky. Swedish children celebrate her feast day on 13th December.

The youngest daughter of each family dresses in a white gown with a blood red sash and wears a crown of evergreen decorated with candles. She wakes her parents and serves them with coffee and special cakes for breakfast.

Christmas candles

Instead of lighting fires to the sun, as pagans had done, Christians lit candles to the Son of God. In medieval times, more than seven hundred years ago, a special candle was lit every night between Christmas Eve and the eve of 6th January. These were the *Twelve Days of Christmas*, when the Christmas festival was held.

Deck the halls

Although Christians did not worship Saturn, they continued the old Roman custom of decorating their homes with evergreens to celebrate the birthday of Jesus.

Holly and Ivy

Holly, one of the most popular evergreens, is a symbol of good luck, just like the horseshoe.

A holly bush planted in the garden is said to keep the house safe from lightning. Farmers used to hang a sprig of holly in their cowsheds on Christmas Eve to make sure they had a good supply of milk and healthy calves during the coming year.

Ivy, which is a soft and clinging plant, was once thought to be a symbol of woman. Holly, with its tough and leathery leaves, was supposed to be a symbol of man. Entwining holly and ivy in a Christmas decoration was supposed to ensure peace in the home between husband and wife in the year ahead.

Christians told stories about the holly to link it with the Christmas story. Even its name reminds us of these stories, for *holly* comes from the same word as *holy*.

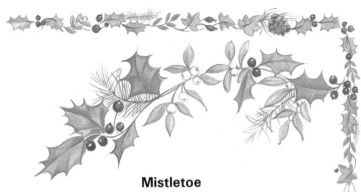

Mistletoe

Mistletoe was a special plant for the Druids, who lived in Britain before the days of Christianity. If it is to flourish, it needs the support of a tree, such as the oak. The oak was a sacred tree to the Druids, who believed that the evergreen mistletoe kept the spirit of the tree alive during the winter months. Mistletoe became a symbol of peace and friendship.

A traditional kissing bush

A *kissing bush* is easy to make – simply cover a framework of hoops with evergreens and hang a sprig of mistletoe from the centre. Any girl who is kissed beneath the bush will be sure of good luck and a happy marriage.

The legend of the Glastonbury thorn

1 After the Crucifixion, Joseph of Arimathea helped to bury Jesus. Then he left Palestine and came to England.

2 Joseph and his followers walked inland to Glastonbury, Somerset, where Joseph stuck his staff into the ground. Immediately, the staff took root and blossomed.

3 Later, a great abbey was built at Glastonbury, but it is now a ruin.

4 Cuttings were taken from the famous old tree before it died. Many of the trees from these survive and some of them still grow in the churchyard at Glastonbury. The thorn trees blossom twice a year, in May and at Christmas. A spray of blossom decorates the Queen's Christmas dinner table.

This is a reconstruction of how Glastonbury Abbey once looked

The miracle of the poinsettia

The Mexicans call the *poinsettia* the 'Flower of the Holy Night', after a legend that tells of a little peasant girl who, on Christmas Eve, wanted to go to Midnight Mass with a gift for Jesus. She had nothing to give, but angels appeared to her and told her to pick some weeds and take them into the cathedral.

As she went in, everyone laughed at her. Suddenly, the top leaves on every stem burst into a flame of scarlet. The people fell to their knees and the little peasant girl marched proudly forward to make her offering at the crib.

Christmas trees

The most popular of all the Christmas evergreens is the *fir tree*. The idea of bringing a fir tree indoors at Christmas is said to have come from Martin Luther, the German religious reformer who lived in the sixteenth century. Fir trees decorated with paper and lights have been popular in Germany ever since.

Martin Luther's tree

Martin Luther brought a fir tree indoors and decorated it with candles to show his children how beautiful the stars had looked one night as he was walking through the forest.

People in England used to grow many kinds of trees in pots for indoor decoration at Christmas. Tiny cherry trees were grown to blossom on Christmas Day.

It was Prince Albert, Queen Victoria's husband, who brought the first Christmas tree over to England from Germany in 1846

Victorian traditions

Many of our Christmas customs are quite new and only became popular during Queen Victoria's reign. Christmas trees, carol singers, Christmas crackers and cards all became popular at this time.

The first Christmas card

In 1843, Sir Henry Cole, realising that he would not find time to write all his letters at Christmas, asked an artist to design a card that he could send to each of his friends. It showed merrymakers making a toast and had a Christmas greeting on the front. But on either side were pictures of the poor being clothed and fed, to remind people that Christmas is a time for remembering those who are in need.

The first Christmas card

Robins have been a popular image on Christmas cards since Victorian times

Christmas crackers

A London sweet shop owner, Tom Smith, invented the first *Christmas cracker* in the 1840s. At first, he sold sugared almonds wrapped in paper, with love mottoes inside. Then he discovered a way of making the wrapping go 'snap' when pulled open. These 'crackers' became so popular that Tom opened a cracker factory to meet the demand.

Advent

Advent begins four weeks before Christmas. It is a time of great anticipation, when Christians look forward to celebrating Christ's birthday.

An *Advent calendar* has twenty four numbered doors, one for every day of Advent. The doors are opened, day by day, to reveal a Christmas scene. The last door is opened on Christmas Eve.

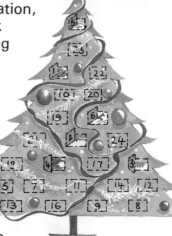

Christmas Eve

Legend says that, at the first chime of midnight on Christmas Eve, animals are able to speak and evil spirits temporarily lose their powers.

The Yule log

In medieval England, the log that burned in the hearth during the Twelve Days of Christmas was called the *Yule log*. Yule is an old word for the winter festival, dating back to Viking times.

Everyone celebrated on Christmas Eve when the Yule log was brought indoors, placed in the hearth and set alight.

Bringing home the Yule log

Snapdragon was once a popular game, played on Christmas Eve. Everyone gathered round as brandy was poured over a bowl of raisins. Then the adults set the brandy alight, the lights were put out and everyone took turns to take a raisin from the flames.

Santa Claus and St Nicholas

All over the world, traditional gift bringers visit children at Christmas. *Santa Claus* is the best known of these. His name comes from the Dutch for 'St Nicholas', which is *Sinterklaas*. St Nicholas was Bishop of Myra, in Asia Minor. He was a rich man who used his wealth to help others. Although his feast day is on 6th December he was so famous for his generosity that his name is always linked with Christmas itself.

In England, the 'spirit of Christmas' was known as Father Christmas

St Nicholas was very popular in the Netherlands and when people from Holland went to live in America they took their love of Sinterklaas with them. Soon, the Americans wanted to share Sinterklaas, and they gave him the new name of Santa Claus.

Santa Claus and his reindeer

It was the Americans who gave Santa Claus a sleigh and a team of reindeer. They named the reindeer *Dasher*, *Dancer*, *Prancer*, *Vixen*, *Comet*, *Cupid*, *Donner* and *Blitzen*. *Rudolph* joined the team later.

Sinterklaas

Dutch children believe that Sinterklaas lives in Spain, where he keeps a big red book in which he writes down all the good and bad deeds of every child.

On 6th December Sinterklaas arrives in Amsterdam in a ship. He rides ashore on a great white horse with his servant, who checks which children have been good before leaving presents for them. That night, Sinterklaas rides across Holland, and children leave out a pair of shoes filled with food for the horse. Sinterklaas leaves little gifts in exchange.

Some of the most popular pictures of St Nicholas were drawn by Thomas Nast in the 1890s. His pictures illustrated a poem called 'A visit from St Nicholas', written in 1822 by Clement C Moore.

A visit from St Nicholas

'Twas the night before Christmas,
      when all through the house
Not a creature was stirring,
      not even a mouse.
The stockings were hung
      by the chimney with care,
In hopes that St Nicholas
      soon would be there;
The children were nestled
      all snug in their beds,
While visions of sugar plums
      danced in their heads...

taken from Clement C Moore's
A visit from St Nicholas

Other gift bringers

Christkindl (Kriss Kringle)

In Germany, the gift bringer is *Christkindl*, the Christ child. On Christmas Eve, children are not allowed to go into the room where the Christmas tree stands. When at last they are allowed in, they are always just too late to catch a glimpse of Christkindl. But there are presents under the tree to show that Christkindl has visited the house.

Befana

Italian children receive gifts on 6th January from an old woman called *Befana*. According to legend, she lived in Bethlehem when Jesus was born. The shepherds told her about the new born child but Befana put off going to visit the baby Jesus and when at last she went to the stable she was too late. Jesus had gone.

It is said that Befana has been wandering all over the world looking for the baby Jesus ever since. She leaves a gift at every house, just in case he is there.

Christmas Day

On Christmas Day, many church services are held to celebrate Jesus's birthday. Some are held after sunset on Christmas Eve, some at midnight, and some take place on Christmas morning.

Christmas fare

Until the sixteenth century, the great Christmas dish for a nobleman was roast wild boar. Other delicacies were peacock, pheasant, capon, swan and goose. For ordinary people, roast goose was the traditional dish for Christmas dinner. Today, turkey is the most popular dish.

A boar's head, with herbs, holly and an apple in its mouth was brought to the table with great ceremony

The *turkey* is a South American bird, and was unknown in Europe until after the Spanish conquest of Mexico. Live turkeys were sent back from Mexico to Spain after 1519, and from Spain they were taken to other parts of Europe.

Roast *peacock* was sometimes served. Cooks prepared the bird by skinning it with all its feathers in place, then stuffing the carcass and roasting it. When the meat was cooked, they put it back into the skin and sewed it up. They sometimes put gilding on the peacock's beak to make it shine. Then they put a wick dipped in alcohol into its mouth, set it alight and carried the bird into the dining hall.

Mince pies

Perhaps you have sometimes wondered what *mincemeat*, which is made from fruits and chopped peel, has to do with meat? The very first mince pies were actually filled with meat that had been shredded into little strips. They were called *shrid pies*.

After 1660 the pies became more like those enjoyed today. They were called *minced pies* and contained a filling of chopped meat and suet (fat from beef and mutton), to which currants, eggs,

Crib pies

Shrid pies were cooked in oblong dishes. During their baking, their crusts would often fall in, making them look like little cribs, or mangers. So cooks would cut a piece of pastry in the shape of a baby and place it on top of the pie before baking. This led to them being called 'crib pies'.

spices, sugar and brandy were added. Eventually, the meat was left out altogether, but mincemeat still has suet in its recipe today.

Wayfarers' pies

The first minced pies were very large. As time went by, cooks began to make them smaller. These were given another name – *wayfarers' pies* – because they were always offered to visitors who called during the Christmas season.

Christmas pudding

The *Christmas pudding* known today began
life as *frumenty*, a dish made of wheat or
corn boiled up in milk. As time went on,
other ingredients, such as prunes, eggs, and
lumps of meat, were added to make it more
interesting. When cooked, it was poured
into a dish and called *plum porridge*.

Later, cooks added even more meat and
suet. They wrapped the mixture up in the
scalded intestines of a pig or sheep and
boiled it like a fat sausage. When cooked,
the pudding could be cut up into slices.

The traditional time for making a Christmas
pudding is 'Stir-up Sunday' at the beginning

Stirring the Christmas pudding

of Advent. A proper Christmas pudding is always stirred from East to West in honour of the three Wise Men. Every member of the family must give the pudding a stir and make a secret wish.

The king's Christmas pudding

There is a legend about how Christmas puddings were invented.

1 One Christmas Eve, a king of England found himself in a forest with no food.

2 Night was drawing on, so he stopped at a woodcutter's cottage and asked for food and shelter.

3 The woodcutter was very poor, but he and the king mixed together all the food they had. The king had only some brandy.

4 The result was a sweet, sticky mixture which they put into a bag and boiled. Lo and behold! They had made the first Christmas pudding!

Telling your fortune in the pudding

Some cooks put silver coins and lucky charms into the pudding mixture. But many years ago, other simple things were added and it became part of the fun to see who got what!

A dried *bean* in your portion meant that you were going to be a king.

A dried *pea* meant that you were going to be a queen.

A *clove* meant that you would grow up to be a rascal.

A *twig* meant that you would grow up to play the fool.

A bit of *rag* in your pudding meant that you were lazy and would rather buy a Christmas pudding than go to the trouble of making one!

Christmas cake

It used to be the custom to bake a special rich cake for Twelfth Night. Today a lighter *Christmas cake* is made and eaten throughout the Christmas period.

Boxing Day

The day after Christmas Day, 26th December, is called Boxing Day. The name goes back to medieval times when alms boxes were placed at the back of every church to collect money for the poor. The alms boxes were always opened on 26th December, which is why it is called Boxing Day.

The idea of alms boxes goes back to Roman times. To pay for their celebrations at the winter festival of the Saturnalia, the Romans used to collect money in little earthenware boxes with a slit in the top.

The Feast of Stephen

Boxing Day is also *St Stephen's Day*. He lived in Rome, and was the first man to be killed for believing in the teachings of Jesus. But some people claim that he shares the day with another St Stephen, who came from Sweden.

St Stephen of Sweden is the patron saint of horses. Boxing Day has long been associated with outdoor sports, especially horse racing and hunting.

Ice skating on Boxing Day, 1860

Racing at Leamington, 1846

New Year

In ancient Rome, people worshipped the god *Janus* at the festival of the New Year. They believed that he had two faces, one looking back at the old year and the other looking forward towards the new. The first month of the year, January, is named after him.

All over the world there are special traditions for 'seeing in the New Year'. In parts of Germany, for instance, there is a custom of dropping molten lead into cold water to see what shapes it makes. The shapes are then 'read', like tea leaves, to foretell the future.

Singing and dancing on New Year's Eve in Ireland, 1870

First footing

In Scotland, where New Year's Eve is called *Hogmanay*, the first person to put a foot across the doorstep in the New Year is said to decide the luck for that household during the coming year.

The 'first footer' should be tall and dark. He should not be flat footed, crosseyed, nor must his eyebrows meet in the middle, for these are all signs of bad luck.

The stranger brings in three lucky objects, usually a piece of coal, a sprig of mistletoe and some money. Without saying a word, he places these on the mantelpiece and wishes everyone a happy New Year.

Afterwards a toast is drunk to absent friends and a traditional song – *Auld Lang Syne* – is sung.

Wassailing

Wassailing was once a popular part of the Christmas celebrations, especially at New Year. On New Year's Eve a wassail bowl was filled with hot spiced ale and passed round.

Twelfth Night

The Christmas festival lasts for twelve days, ending with Twelfth Night or the *Feast of the Epiphany*, when Christians remember the three Wise Men, who came to visit Jesus at Bethlehem.

Gifts from the Wise Men

Each of the gifts from the three Wise Men had a special meaning. *Gold* was given because it is a symbol of royalty. *Frankincense* was given because it is a symbol of God and *myrrh* because it is a symbol of suffering.

Twelfth Night is still an important part of the Christmas holiday in some European countries, even though this custom has died out in Britain. There are parties and presents and in Spain children leave out their shoes, hoping that the three Wise Men will fill them with presents when they pass by.

A family party on Twelfth Night

Burning the Christmas decorations

King or Queen for a day

In England, it used to be traditional to bake a Twelfth Night cake with a single bean in it. The person who found the bean in their slice of cake could be *Bean King* or *Queen* for a day, and could choose a partner to help them to rule over the celebrations.

Christmas merrymaking in Tudor times at Haddon Hall, Derbyshire

The Lord of Misrule

During medieval times, someone was chosen to be the *Lord of Misrule* for the Twelve Days of Christmas. It was his job to plan all the Christmas festivities – plays, games and songs.

Fruit tree wassailing

Fruit tree wassailing often took place on Twelfth Night. The wassail bowl was filled with cider, and when everyone had taken a drink, the cider was sprinkled on the fruit trees. Guns were then fired through the branches of the trees.

Pantomimes

Pantomimes have now become part of a traditional English Christmas. The word *pantomime* means *all mime*.

In early pantomimes, the story was told by traditional characters, such as Harlequin. No words were used and the story was acted out entirely through dancing and mime. Early pantomimes were usually about the myths and legends of gods and heroes. But from the mid eighteenth century onwards they were based on folk and fairy tales, such as *Jack and the Beanstalk* or *Dick Whittington*. Today, pantomimes tell their stories in a mixture of words, song and dance.

English pantomimes

It is traditional in English pantomime for a man to play the dame (usually 'she' is the hero's mother) and for a girl to play the handsome young hero. In pantomime, everything is topsy turvy, but good always wins over evil and everything turns out happily in the end.

A Christmas pantomime

In 1806, a famous clown called Joseph Grimaldi appeared at Covent Garden in *Mother Goose*. He made the audience laugh so much with his acrobatics and his *slapstick* – a stick made to give a loud *crack!* whenever he hit another character with it – that later pantomimes always contained some 'slapstick' comedy.

41

Christmas around the world

In some parts of the world 25th December falls in the middle of summer. In Australia and New Zealand, people still eat the traditional Christmas dinner of turkey and pudding, but they sometimes eat cold meat, salads and fresh fruit as well.

In Mexico, there is one particular Christmas custom specially for children. An earthenware jar called a *piñata* is filled with sweets, nuts and fruit, decorated with gold and silver paper and coloured streamers, and then hung from the ceiling.

Christmas is a time for carnivals on the Pacific island of Micronesia

The children take it in turns to try to break the piñata with a stick in order to get at the good things inside.

Christmas celebrations in Bethlehem

'A Merry Christmas'

in different languages

French	Joyeux Noël!	**Turkish**	Noeliniz kutlu olsun!
German	Fröhliche Weihnachten!	**Irish**	Nollaig faoi shéan agus faoi shonas duit!
Spanish	Felices Pascuas!		
Italian	Buon Natale!	**Norwegian**	Gledelig Jul!
Welsh	Nadolig Llawen!	**Dutch**	Vrolijk Kerstmis!

INDEX